Hello there, what's your name? I'm Mother Forest.
I can't remember my age exactly, but I must be at
least a billion years old. I have lots of things to show you.
Would you like to come for a walk with me?

Remember to keep your eyes open, and mind where you step.
My home is huge and there are sure to be surprises in store.
Do you want to choose where to go to next?

To head north, turn to page 2.
To take the path leading south, head to page 3.

Cuckoo! Cuckoo! Who's that singing?
It's the cuckoo, of course.

Some people say that if you have a penny
in your pocket the first time you hear a
cuckoo sing, it will bring you good luck.

Now, let's keep moving.
To go deep into the heart of the forest,
turn to page 4.

KNOCK! KNOCK!
KNOCK!

Knock, knock! Who's there? Look up! Can you see?
It's the green woodpecker, hunting for tiny insects
that are hidden in the bark of the tree.
You can hear him knocking from far away
if you listen carefully.

Look, there's a squirrel! Let's follow it to page 5.
Or would you rather discover the world of insects?
Then go to page 9.

Watch out, there's a wild boar over there! She's always hungry and likes to root around in the earth looking for things to eat. Be careful: she doesn't like to be disturbed and might charge if she sees you. Oh no, here she comes!

Quick, climb up that tree to page 6!
Or run as fast as you can to page 11.

Just as I thought, the squirrel has scampered home to this
big oak tree. Trees are very precious things. Their wood can be
used to build houses, make furniture or to burn as fuel to keep warm.
Do you know that trees can be tasty too? Maple syrup is just one
delicious thing that comes from a tree.

Would you like a drink of water? Then go to the waterfall on page 7.
Otherwise, let's keep strolling to page 12.

5

We're safe now, high up in a tree.
Let me introduce you to the sparrowhawk.
It's a bird of prey, a bird that hunts other
animals for its food. It spots its prey from
high up in the sky and swoops down to catch it.

To climb on to its back,
hold on tight and turn to page 8.
Or put your feet back on the ground
and follow the path to page 10.

6

4

Here we are. Sit down by the waterfall for a moment and take a few sips of its clean, fresh water. Lots of animals and birds come here to drink, especially at sunrise or sunset.

Now we're well rested, let's go and discover the world of insects on page 9.

Can you imagine a more wonderful view than this, riding on the back of a bird! You can see all the different shades of the seasons laid out below. In the winter, the forest wears a cloak of snow, before the new leaves and beautiful flowers of springtime arrive. In the summer, the paths are full of fruits and flowers, and then the autumn leaves turn the trees red, orange and yellow.

Listen, can you hear a strange sound?
What can it be? Let's go to page 10 and find out.

8

Two of the big insects look
exactly the same as each other.
Can you spot them? Warning:
the little ones don't count!

Look at these creepy-crawly creatures! Under the stones, the trunks, the moss, the leaves... every little corner of the forest is filled with them. Did you know that insects are some of the most useful animals there are? They help plants grow by taking pollen from one flower to the next.

To go even deeper into the forest, turn to page 11. If you prefer to stay on the path, go to page 12.

To go even deeper into the forest, turn to page 11. If you prefer to stay on the path, go to page 12.

9

What's that noise? Is it a wolf? Is it a bear?
No, it's a stag, bellowing! He's looking for a female
deer to start a family. Stags lose their antlers when
winter ends, but they grow back every year.
If you look carefully, you might find old antlers
on the ground. Can you see any?

Let's leave the deer in peace and continue to page 13.

10

Look, it's a family of badgers. Did you know, when they're not wandering around the forest looking for food, badgers make their home in a network of tunnels underground. This home is called a sett. It can have as many as forty entrances, but they hide them so well, you hardly ever see them.

Go to page 14 for the next stage in your journey.

To-whit! To-whoo! Who's that hooting?
It's a pair of owls, hidden in the trees.
Owls sleep during the day, then come out at
night to hunt for food by the light of the moon.

Oh! I didn't realize how late it is.
It's time to go home. Don't worry:
I know the way. Follow me to page 15.

13

Shush! Don't make a sound! These foxes are hunting for their dinner. They approach their prey slowly before they suddenly pounce.

Do you know what time it is? It's getting late and it's about to turn dark. Come on, let's take the path home to page 15.

You made it! What a fun time we've had.
Feel free to come back whenever you want
some fresh forest air. If you'd like to meet again
for another adventure, all you have to do is
open the book at page 1 and choose your path.

See you soon!